Dedicated to my Pep,
who never judged
and considered
everyone a friend.

This book is given with love:

To: _____

From: _____

May we not just learn
life's most important lessons,
but live them.
Pay more attention to our people.
Take time to rest.
Find joy in the little things.

May you sit longer with those
who make you happy.
Stay awhile in the places
that bring you joy.
And love greater than yesterday,
for the days go fast.

Book 2

SIT. STAY. LOVE.

Be the Bestest Kind of Friend

Written by: Chalaine Kilduff   Illustrated by: Sally Brodermann

The world is a great big place,
right outside our door.

So many friends to meet,
and so much to explore.

Me? I love the flowers
and how they sway in the breeze.

Or a nice, shaded nap
right below the willow trees.

I love playing in the sun
and seeing a bird as it flies.

There's beauty everywhere you look
if you just direct your eyes.

But if you want to know
what I love most about this place...

It's that it's full of different people,
there's always a new face!

Faces to meet and faces to love.
Faces all made from God up above.

So many faces that God sends your way...
So many friends to adventure and play.

And here's my advice,
if I could make one request...

Don't just be a good friend,
be the best of the best!

Start by learning how to love.
I'll tell you how to lead...

Look around and recognize
we're all of the same breed.

No matter where you come from
or the history of your name,

We may look different,
but as God's children, we're all the same.

It doesn't matter how we look,
what's our color or our size.

It's what's in our hearts that matters,
not what you see with your eyes.

It's our job to be loving
to all those that we meet.

When it comes to our table,
everyone deserves a seat.

So go out there and show
the world how it's done.

When life seems a little dark,
bring it some sun.

Be nice to everyone -
no matter what they have
or what they lack.

Because we're one big family,
all part of the same pack!

ABOUT THE AUTHOR

Chalaine Kilduff has been a storyteller since she could talk.

Working in advertising, she's written for countless clients from global brands to small town businesses. Her work has been printed in magazines, played as TV commercials and posted on Times Square billboards.

With a passion for piecing together words that matter and make a difference, she continues to follow God's calling on what to pen. Now, she's fulfilled a dream to become a published author, entering the children's book space with a goal to provide fun characters and faith-centered content that helps kids learn important lessons as they grow up.

Chalaine currently lives in a small New England town where she serves as a first lady. Married to the mayor, her and her hubby recently upped their parent game, welcoming a beautiful baby girl as a sister to their lovable Fox Red Labrador.
You can find her taking lots of puppy pics, tackling life as a new mom and traveling as much as possible at @chaleezy.

THE AUTHOR'S INSPIRATION

For as long as I can remember, I've been a writer. My parents have pages filled with messy penmanship and misspelled stories I made up as a little girl. I practiced my signature in countless notepads wishing for a future where I'd get asked for my autograph. Only God could have made that wish come true.

Starting this series is truly living out a dream. A dream that many helped make happen. This book is dedicated to one of my biggest supporters - my dear Pep, who drove me to school many mornings and paid for countless breakfasts when I barely had two pennies to rub together.

My Pep always had a joke to share and a wave to give. He never knew a stranger and considered everyone a friend. "Scotty," as he was fondly known, loved to visit his favorite local diner each day and strike up a conversation with anyone the Lord passed his way.

This book is for him. May we all have a little "Pep" in our step.

And may we all live a little more like my Lab. This book is in honor of him. Jeter, my fluffy, big-headed and floppy-eared yellow Labrador changed my life in the best ways possible - and then cancer stole him from me.

Sit. Stay. Love. is a tribute to my sweet pup who taught me so many lessons, and who now continues teaching through this series...

MEET THE ILLUSTRATOR

After a long career as a Graphic Designer, Sally decided to become a full-time freelance illustrator. She went from working alongside a team every day to working with a trio of cats at her home office - and she wouldn't trade it for the world. She considers it an absolute joy to wake up every morning and draw until her heart's content.

Raised by artists, her parents were both amazingly talented. Her dad painted incredibly detailed steam trains and her Mum was a textile artist. She grew up drawing and creating and considers herself to be taught by the best. To this day, her Mum continues to be her biggest fan (and harshest critic!).

Sally lives in a quaint village in the UK with her husband and cats where they often welcome a favorite and constant visitor - a huge yellow Labrador named Roger. Roger and their cats (Wally, Milly and Sylvester) are her inspiration. When she's not drawing, you can find her spending time in her garden or walking the Oxfordshire countryside. Follow her work @sallybrodermann - but don't expect to see any real photos, because she hates having her photo taken!

SIT. STAY. LOVE.
THE SERIES

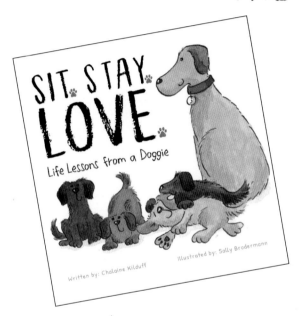

We train dogs, but they teach us.
And we have so much to learn.

Collect the books from the sweetest
and cuddliest series there is.
Follow these furry friends along
for even more fun @sitstayloveseries

Claim your FREE Gift!

 Visit:

PDICBooks.com/Gift

Thank you for purchasing

SIT. STAY. LOVE.

and welcome to the Puppy Dogs & Ice Cream family.
We're certain you're going to love the little gift
we've prepared for you at the website above.

Meet the
SIT. STAY. LOVE.
Family

Meet the pups who are here to help you learn and grow.
They teach the kind of lessons everyone should know.

They believe the world can be better because of you.
Just imagine all the good that we can do!

This pack is made up of the best as they come –
Really, there's no one better to learn from!

Apollo

Jete

Ruckus

Otto

Hink

Walz